COUNTING SHEEP

CALPURNIA TATE ❧ GIRL VET

COUNTING SHEEP

BY **JACQUELINE KELLY**

WITH ILLUSTRATIONS BY JENNIFER L. MEYER

GODWIN BOOKS

HENRY HOLT AND COMPANY · NEW YORK

HENRY HOLT AND COMPANY

Publishers since 1866

175 Fifth Avenue, New York, New York 10010

mackids.com

Henry Holt® is a registered trademark of Macmillan Publishing Group, LLC.

Text copyright © 2017 by Jacqueline Kelly

Illustrations copyright © 2017 by Jennifer L. Meyer

Library of Congress Cataloging-in-Publication Data

Names: Kelly, Jacqueline, author. | Meyer, Jennifer L., illustrator.

Title: Counting sheep : Calpurnia Tate, girl vet /

Jacqueline Kelly ; illustrated by Jennifer L. Meyer.

Description: First edition. | New York : Henry Holt and Company, 2017. |

Series: Calpurnia Tate, girl vet | Summary: In rural Texas in 1901,

thirteen-year-old Callie nurses a butterfly with a broken wing and delivers a baby lamb,

despite her mother's disapproval of Callie's "unladylike behavior."

Identifiers: LCCN 2016002104 (print) | LCCN 2016028637 (ebook)

ISBN 9781627798709 (hardback) | ISBN 9781627798716 (Ebook)

Subjects: | CYAC: Veterinarians—Fiction. | Naturalists—Fiction. |

Sex role—Fiction. | Family life—Texas—Fiction. |

Texas—History—1846–1950—Fiction. | BISAC: JUVENILE FICTION / Animals /

General. | JUVENILE FICTION / Historical / United States / 20th Century.

Classification: LCC PZ7.K296184 Co 2017 (print) | LCC PZ7.K296184 (ebook) |

DDC [Fic]—dc23

LC record available at https://lccn.loc.gov/2016002104

Our books may be purchased in bulk for promotional, educational,

or business use. Please contact your local bookseller or the Macmillan

Corporate and Premium Sales Department at (800) 221-7945 ext. 5442

or by e-mail at MacmillanSpecialMarkets@macmillan.com.

First Edition—2017 / Designed by April Ward

Printed in the United States of America by LSC Communications, Harrisonburg, Virginia

1   3   5   7   9   10   8   6   4   2

For animal lovers everywhere

What I'm going to tell you about took place on our farm in Fentress, Texas, in the early spring of 1901. Now, if you don't live on a farm, you might not know that spring is the season when most of the animals have their babies, and places like ours were

overrun with lambs and calves and piglets and kittens. Most of these babies were born without any trouble, but sometimes things would go wrong. That's when you'd call Dr. Pritzker for help.

Dr. Pritzker was our town's animal doctor. (The fancy word for this is *veterinarian*.) Even though I was only thirteen, Dr. Pritzker and I became friends, and sometimes he'd let me help in his office making labels for the medicines he used. Sometimes—even better—he'd let me read his books, and I learned about the various diseases of livestock. And other times—best of all— he'd let me watch when he doctored the animals. Mother didn't like this. She thought it wasn't ladylike or proper, and for some reason she was dead set on me being ladylike and proper. I don't

know why; it didn't look like much fun to me. So I didn't usually tell her about it. To be truthful, I almost never told her about it. I figured I was doing her a kindness by sparing her from things that made her unhappy, right?

Right.

Our farmhouse was really big, which was a good thing since it was filled to bursting with Mother and Father and Granddaddy and me and a total of six brothers. Yep, six. And when you're the only girl, six brothers is far too many. About five too many. I've said it before and I'll say it again: Life is just not fair sometimes.

Out of all my too-many brothers, I was closest to Travis, who was only a year younger. Travis, with his soft heart and sunny smile, was crazy about animals. *All* animals. He raised rabbits as pets in the dark corner of the barn, and he was so tender, he got upset whenever we killed a turkey at Thanksgiving or even a chicken for Sunday dinner. Honestly, that boy needed to toughen up. Like me.

I was spending the morning looking for black-spotted newts in the shallows

of the San Marcos River near our house and making a fine muddy job of it. Newts are shy creatures, and I was having no luck. I'd always wanted to raise one because they live part of their lives in the water like tadpoles, then lose their gills, grow legs, and walk about on the land. A pretty good trick, if you ask me.

Way off in the distance, I heard our cook, Viola, ringing the bell to signal lunch. Uh-oh. I'd wandered farther than I meant to, and now I'd be late to the table. This was considered very bad manners in our house and much frowned upon. I took off running.

By the time I made it to the back door, the family was seated in the dining room and Viola was ferrying plates through the swinging door to the table. I took a quick look at myself in the kitchen mirror. The mirror reflected a red face streaked with dirt and hair damp with sweat.

Viola, dishing up the potatoes, said, "You look like a boiled beet."

I splashed my face under the kitchen pump to cool down.

"Not much of an improvement," she said. "Now you look like a drowned rat."

"Ha. So funny."

"Don't forget to wash those filthy paws."

I scrubbed my hands with the rough kitchen soap. "Is she mad?"

She meaning Mother, of course.

"What d'you think?" Viola picked up a clean dish towel. "Here. Come here." She daubed at my face. "That's better. Go." She flapped the towel at me.

I slid into the dining room, torn between standing tall to maintain my dignity or slinking in like a wet, smelly dog. But either way, it didn't matter. There was no dignity; there was no hiding. Mother stared at me coldly, and the room fell silent. I slipped into my chair next to Travis.

"Well, Calpurnia," said Mother, "what is the meaning of this?"

"Sorry, Mother," I whispered.

"You look like you've been digging in the mud. Why is that?"

"Because I've been digging in the mud, of course."

Oops. What I said was true, but the way I had said it turned out to be not so smart.

"Take your plate to the kitchen, young lady," said Mother. "You may join us at dinner, if you are clean by

then and have learned some manners."

My older brother Lamar snickered. I shot him a dirty look and carried my plate out.

Viola and I sat across from each other at the kitchen table, which was okay with me. She could be good company when she wasn't in one of her moods. And the smell of her fried chicken filled the kitchen. I considered it the best smell in the whole world.

"You mouth off again?" she said.

There was no need to reply. The answer was sitting in front of her. I attacked my chicken with both hands, one of the benefits of eating in the kitchen. Eating in the dining room meant you had to wrestle your chicken from your plate to your mouth with a knife and fork, always a tricky exercise.

"Mmm, Viola," I said, through a big bite, "this is the best chicken ever."

"Thank you kindly. And don't talk with your mouth full. I don't wanna see that."

"Ummpf."

For dessert there was chocolate pecan pie with fresh cream. Viola cut me a slice that was a tiny bit bigger than

the others and gave me an extra splash of cream. Another good thing about eating in the kitchen. When I tried to thank her, she pretended to have no idea what I was talking about.

After lunch I changed into a clean pinafore and went in search of Granddaddy. I found him in the library packing up the collecting jars and field guides in his satchel.

"Where are we going today?" I said.

"We'll cross the bridge and follow the trail through the pecan grove. Are

you allowed to come with me? I thought perhaps your mother might have banished you to your room."

"She probably meant to," I admitted, "but I think she just forgot." This seemed to be the only good thing about

all these brothers: There were so many of us that Mother couldn't always keep track of who was misbehaving and in what way.

"No need to remind her," I said.

"No need at all." He gathered up his bag and walking stick, I grabbed my butterfly net, and off we went.

Not everybody in town knew it, but my grandfather was a Scientist and the smartest man in maybe all of Texas. I could ask him anything about anything; he always knew the answer, but he wouldn't always tell me. He had this habit of making me figure things out for myself. But that's all right; he didn't do it to be annoying. He was just trying to make me smarter (which clearly was working since I was the smartest kid around, although my teacher, Miss Harbottle, might have disagreed).

We crossed the bridge and turned onto a mule deer trail on the far side of the river. They were called mule deer because of their huge ears. If we were

very lucky, we might see a mother deer with her new fawn. But such sights were rare. You could be standing right next to a mule deer and never know it unless it flicked an ear or twitched its tail. And Nature painted the  fawn with spots that turned it invisible in the undergrowth, protecting it from predators.

We didn't come across a fawn, but we

did find a porcupine, or rather the back half of a porcupine. It had heard us coming and tried to burrow into a hole in the riverbank, but the hole was too shallow and its hind end stuck out. Still, it was safe. No animal in its right mind would go near those quills, even if they were only half the usual number.

"Ah," said Granddaddy, "*Erethizon dorsatum,* meaning the animal with the irritating back."

I knew this was the Scientific name. It sounded a whole lot fancier than what some folks called them, namely prickle pig and quill pig and thorny hog. And as for "irritating"? Ha! That was an understatement.

Granddaddy went on, "The quills are actually a form of modified hairs."

"Is it true that they can shoot them at you?"

"Sometimes when the animal shakes itself, the loose quills will fly off, giving rise to the folktale that it can actually aim and fire at will. That is nonsense. If one of those quills hits you, it is by sheer chance. One must normally touch the animal for the quill to embed itself in the flesh. But once embedded, the barbed end will work itself deeper and deeper with every twitch of the unhappy victim. If it pierces a vital area, the victim may die. They live on vegetation and the bark of trees and are very good climbers."

The porcupine lashed its tail as a warning. Even though it couldn't aim at me, I stood well back.

Granddaddy went on, "You don't

normally see them during the day, because they are nocturnal. The young are called porcupettes. They are born with soft quills that harden into service within an hour of birth."

Porcupettes. Travis would like that; I'd have to remember to tell him. Or maybe not. He'd probably want to bring one home. Just what we needed, another disastrous pet.

We wisely left the porcupine alone and wandered along the trail, stopping to look at beetles and butterflies along the way.

I examined a leaf that had

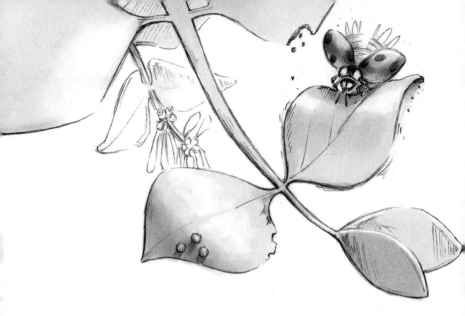

three tiny pale green globs the size of pinheads attached to it. "Look, Granddaddy, what are these?"

"What do you think they are?"

I sighed. "You could just tell me about it, you know, like the porcupine. Instead here you are doing it again."

"Doing what again?"

"Making me think for myself."

"Why, yes. Is that a complaint?"

"Oh no no no no no." I studied the shiny little globs. "Maybe it's some kind of disease on the leaf. No, I think they look more like eggs of some sort, insect eggs. They're too small for anything else."

A bright orange butterfly with black-and-white patches flitted past. A Painted Lady. Not a rare butterfly but a pretty one. Maybe these were her very own eggs.

"I hope they're butterfly eggs. I'm going to raise them and see what they turn into."

I gently put the leaf into a collecting jar. ("Collecting jar" makes it sound grander than it really was, which is to say a Ball canning jar I'd filched from Viola and then punched some holes in the lid with a nail.)

3

A couple of days later, I woke up to find that the three tiny pale green dots were indeed eggs that had turned into three tiny pale green caterpillars, so small that I had to borrow Granddaddy's magnifying glass to study them. They set to work munching on their leaf. Over the next few days, they grew larger and developed white spots along their sides. Then they shed their skins. Then they started to grow bristles. I made a note in my Scientific Notebook: Caterpillars now longer and fatter. Have shed their skins. Granddaddy says this is called the "instar" stage. Says they will shed a total of five times before they even begin to start turning into butterflies. Seems like a whole lot of work to me.

Travis agreed with me about that. Every few days, I let him come into my room and use the magnifier with me to

follow their progress. (But of course he didn't keep a Scientific Notebook like me. That boy was far too dreamy to buckle down for Science.)

By now the caterpillars were quite fat and almost two inches long. I had borrowed one of Granddaddy's field

guides and identified them for sure as Painted Ladies, or *Vanessa cardui*.

For their next stage, they climbed to the lid of the jar and hung head downward in curved shapes like fishhooks. They molted one last time and this time turned into gray-brown pupae. Then they stopped moving.

The field guide said they would emerge in ten days. So ten days later, I started checking on them all day long, but the first two hatched when I was at school and I missed the whole thing. Should I plead illness and stay home to catch the third one for sure? Mother

would probably dose me with cod liver oil, the worst-tasting stuff in the whole world. Was it worth it? I was trying to decide when the third one made up its mind for me.

The pupa shook on its stem and then slowly split open. Out crawled a brand-new butterfly, its wings damp and crumpled. Over the next half hour, it slowly spread its wings as far as it could to dry them. So now I had three Painted Ladies crammed in the jar, and it was a pretty tight fit. They didn't look too happy. I'd have to let them go.

I carried the jar out to the barn

where Travis was brushing Bunny, his giant white Angora rabbit. Bunny was shedding his winter coat, and little clouds of white fur drifted through the air. The barn kittens watched with interest, swatting and leaping at the floating clouds and tumbling over each other.

"Look what I've got." I showed him the jar full of orange wings. "Time to let them go."

"Can't you keep them? You could keep them if you found a bigger jar."

"No," I said, "they only live for a few weeks."

"Gosh, that seems a shame."

"Plus they've got lots of work to do before they die. They have to lay eggs so that there'll always be more Painted Ladies around."

We admired the riot of color in the jar a little longer and then walked out into the sunlight. I opened the jar and two of them crawled out, opening and stretching their wings and uncurling their antennae. I'd expected them to take off and disappear right away, but they didn't. They made a few fluttery trial flights of a couple of feet, I guess to get the feel of their wings. The last

butterfly crawled out and perched on the lip of the jar. One of its wings looked kind of, well, funny.

As if reading my mind, Travis said, "That one looks kind of funny."

One wing looked fine, but the other was bent and broken. Oh no. Was it just born that way, or was it broken because I'd kept it in a jar that was too small? In which case it was my fault. In which case I should try to do something about it. But what? Could I go to Dr. Pritzker with an insect? Even though he was my friend, he'd probably laugh me out of his office. I could hear him saying, "It's only a butterfly. You can't spend your time trying to fix one butterfly."

True, it was only one butterfly. But think of all the eggs it would lay, and all of *those* butterflies, and then all of *their* eggs, and then all of *those* butterflies, an endless chain of Painted Ladies stretching off into the future for years, for centuries. So at that very moment, I held in my hand not only a single *present* butterfly but a million *future* butterflies.

All right. There was only one possible answer to my problem: Granddaddy.

I said, "I'm going to consult with Granddaddy. If anyone knows what to do, he will."

I gently nudged the insect back in the jar and carried it to the library. I knocked on the door and heard the familiar reply: "Enter if you must."

I entered the dim room and shut the door behind me. I didn't want any of my brothers—besides Travis, of course—knowing about this or they'd think me crazy and I'd never hear the end of it. Lamar especially would tease me until the end of time, and his teasing was not the fun, playful kind but the cruel, hateful kind.

Granddaddy sat reading *A History of the Dinosaurs in Texas*. The word *dinosaur* means "terrible lizard." How could you

not be interested in a creature with a name like that? According to Granddaddy, they weren't truly lizards, but they'd lived so long ago we weren't exactly sure what they were. Some swam in the sea, some galloped on the ground, some flew in the air. Granddaddy said some of them were bigger than our house. Now, this was hard to believe, but he would never fib about something like that. (In fact, he never fibbed about anything. You could count on him for the facts.)

He put down his book and said, "What have you got there?"

"It's the last Painted Lady. I let the other ones go, but there's something wrong with this one."

"Let's take a look." He opened a drawer and pulled out one of his magnifying glasses, the one with the lens as big as a saucer. He peered at the butterfly, and I almost giggled because the lens magnified not only the insect but his blue eye as well, making it the size of a baseball. "The right forewing is broken. Here," he said, handing me the magnifier.

I looked through the glass. The wing looked huge. And the tear in the wing that looked so tiny with the naked eye now looked like a giant rip. "Do you think we can, uh, fix it?" Even as I said it, I felt a bit silly.

But thank goodness he didn't laugh at me. "How do you propose we do that?"

Oh, good. He'd said "we," which meant he was going to help me.

"Well, I guess we need to glue the crack together somehow or make a splint across the gap. But it will have to be very light and small."

"You're right. What sort of material will we use?"

"Um . . . perhaps a toothpick?"

"A whole toothpick?"

"That would probably be too long and too heavy. Perhaps just a tiny part of one?"

In the hall, Viola rang the gong at the foot of the stairs to signal dinner in five minutes. I sighed. It seemed like my time with Granddaddy was always being interrupted by stupid things, like meals.

"I propose that we both think on it," said Granddaddy, "and discuss it again tomorrow after lunch. Is that convenient for you?"

"Oh, absolutely." I ran upstairs to my room with the patient, washed my face and hands, and just made it to the table in time. Travis was bursting to ask me about it, I could tell, but we had to wait for Father to say the blessing.

As we ate, Travis and I talked quietly about my plans for a toothpick splint and how I was really doing it for the many generations of butterflies to come.

"But don't tell the others," I said. "They'll only think it's stupid."

"I don't think it's stupid,

Callie. I think it's really smart of you to figure it out."

"Thanks, but I don't know for sure it will work. I'll do my best, but I can't make any promises."

T he next day after lunch, I met
Granddaddy in the library.

"Ah," he said, "I see you have our
patient. For such fine work, we will
need more light."

He pulled back the green velvet
drapes, and light flooded the gloomy

room. Then he lit four lamps and set them on the corners of his desk. I'd never seen the room so bright.

"Put the patient in the middle," he said.

I set the jar in the middle of the desk next to the items he had assembled: an old soft washrag, a loop of fine wire, a handful of toothpicks, tweezers, scissors, and a bottle of glue. Along with, of course, his magnifying glass.

"I can tell what all these things are for," I said, "except for the wire."

"That's to hold our *Vanessa* still. You'll see in a moment."

46

I opened the jar. He reached in and gently pinched the butterfly's wings closed between thumb and forefinger. He pulled it out and set it down on the washrag. Then, when the butterfly opened its wings, he took the loop of wire and set it across the wings to hold them still without crushing them.

"There you are," he said. "It's all ready for you."

"Me?" I squeaked. "But I thought we were doing this together."

"We *are* doing this together. Do you not see me standing here before you, or am I merely a ghost? I shall hold the magnifying glass for you while you repair the wing."

"Uh, why don't I hold the magnifying glass while *you* repair the wing?"

"Calpurnia, I have complete faith in your abilities. Now. Is the light adequate?"

"Um, I guess."

"Kindly do not guess. It either is or it isn't, in which case I shall light another lamp for you."

"No no, it's fine."

"Then cut a length of toothpick just slightly longer than the gap in the wing. If you make it too long, it will weigh the insect down. If you make it too short, it won't hold when it attempts to fly."

Granddaddy held the glass, and I peered through it. The legs and antennae squirmed a little, but the wings were still. I grasped a toothpick with the tweezers and placed it alongside the broken wing—it looked as big as a log

through the glass, and I felt like Gulliver on his travels when he was shipwrecked in a land of giants.

"Here," said Granddaddy, handing me the scissors.

I cut a tiny length of the "log," about one-eighth of an inch, then measured it against the rip.

"That looks right to me," I said.

"Good. Now put a little—a very little—glue on it. Use another toothpick to apply it as thinly as possible, and be very careful. If you get glue anywhere else on the insect, that will be the end of it."

Granddaddy's hand held steady. My

hand shook a little, which under the magnifier turned into big jerky movements. I took a deep breath, and my hand held still. I managed to dab some glue on my splint, but Granddaddy looked at it and shook his head. "Too much glue. Do you see how it's oozing off the end there? Cut another length and try again."

I held my breath, measured, and cut again, but this time the toothpick splintered.

"Once more," he said, "and Calpurnia, there's no rush. Take your time. When faced with such fine fiddly work, it's best to take your time."

Another toothpick, another cut, and this time the splint looked just right. I even managed to get the right amount of glue on it.

"That's good," said Granddaddy. "Now comes the difficult part."

What? What had I been doing if not the difficult part?

"You will only have one chance to place the splint across the gap on the wing. If you put it in the wrong place, if you get glue in the wrong place, the wing is ruined and it will never fly again."

He didn't have to tell me what that meant.

All right, Calpurnia, I told myself, *here we go.*
I looked through the glass and held the
splint with the tweezers above the gap. I
took a deep breath and held it. And then,
when my hand was as steady as it was ever
going to be, I gently lowered it onto the
wing. Was it in the right place? It looked
like the right place to me. I was still holding my breath. I glanced anxiously at
Granddaddy for confirmation.

"Well done," he said.

I let out a great whoosh of air and
gasped for breath. "Whew. That's a
relief."

"We must let the glue dry well, and
then we shall see."

53

He returned to his book. I didn't take my eyes off the *Vanessa*. The room was silent but for the ticktock of the mantel clock.

Ten minutes later he looked up and said, "Are you ready to test your handiwork? Let's take it outside and see how it goes."

"Yessir. But first I have to fetch Travis to watch this. He's part of it, you see."

We agreed to meet at Mother's flower garden in five minutes. Granddaddy gently put our patient back in its jar, and I took off in search of Travis.

He wasn't in his room, and he wasn't in the barn, and I was about to give up on him when he came out of the woods that led down to the river, holding a small box turtle.

"Come on, Travis," I shouted. "We're going to let the Painted Lady go. And put that turtle down. You don't need another one, and neither do I."

He put the turtle on the ground, pointed it in the direction of the river, and trotted up to join me.

"Did you fix it?" he said.

"I hope so. But there's only one way to find out."

We found Granddaddy waiting for us among the roses and lilies. "Ah, young man, have you come to assist with the launch?"

"Yessir," Travis said shyly. He didn't spend time with Granddaddy and always seemed a little afraid of him. Not like me.

Granddaddy handed me the jar and said, "Since you saved it, I think you should do the honors."

Vanessa fluttered a little. Oh dear. Would the wing hold under the stress of flight? I opened the jar, and the butterfly crawled up to the lip and rested there for a moment, stretching its wings.

Then it took off flying. And flew three feet. And landed on Travis's palm.

"Look," he whispered.

"Shhh," I said.

"Hold still," said Granddaddy.

Travis held still. It was a magical moment. The butterfly slowly opened

and closed its wings, each time show-
ing us the tiny splint. I'll never forget
my brother standing there, the look of
wonder on his face at the living scrap of
sunshine he held in his hand.

After several seconds the butterfly
took off, and although its flight was a
little wobbly, it was indeed flying. It
headed for a honeysuckle vine to feed
on the nectar.

"Congratulations, Calpurnia," said
Granddaddy, "you have successfully
launched your patient. Now if you'll
both excuse me, I have some reading to
catch up on."

"Wow," said Travis, "that was really something."

"You're lucky," I said. "I've never had one land on me."

"You did something better. You saved it."

We watched it sipping the honeysuckle nectar. We were just turning to go when a sudden angry buzz filled the air. A Rufous hummingbird with a bright orange chest zipped through the garden. We had seen him before. He had wintered over in the garden and no doubt looked upon the vine as his own private property. Before Travis

and I could act, he charged at our butterfly. It was Rufous versus Vanessa, two airborne orange dots buzzing and flitting and tumbling through the air. Vanessa took sudden evasive action, and my heart clenched, fearful that my splint would fail it. Even though Rufous was one of the world's smallest birds, he was much fiercer and faster and could hover and fly backward and upside down (which, as far as I know, a

butterfly could not do). He buzzed it again. He didn't actually hit it, but he succeeded in scaring it off to the nearest lily, thirty feet away. Thank goodness he seemed happy enough with this and did not pursue it.

"Whew," said Travis, "that was a close one. That bird almost wrecked it. All

your work could have gone down the drain."

I caught a glimpse of it the next day, and I'm sure because I could see the splint. After that I never saw it again. But I like to think it flew safely into the bushes and found a mate and laid many eggs. I like to think that every time I saw a Painted Lady on our property that it was one of its—and my—descendants.

Unlike Vanessa, most of the livestock on our farm did not have a
name. But there was one sheep that
did. Her name was Snow White, and
she was Mother's favorite out of all our
many animals. Snow White's wool was
the softest in the county, not itchy

against the skin at all, and won prizes at the Fall Fair every year. Mother had the hired man shear her twice a year and sold the wool for a goodly sum. She worried about her and would even go to her pen to pet her and feed her little treats of apples and carrots, something she never bothered to do with any other animal. Snow White's wool was in such demand that Mother had decided to breed her and sell the lamb. By spring, Snow White grew big and round.

On a Saturday morning, Mother sent Travis and me out to her pen next to the barn with an extra ration of grain. But she refused the food and

pawed restlessly at the straw scattered about, mounding it in the corner.

"Look," said Travis, "she's making a nest."

"It won't be long now." The sheep lay down in the hay, and I said to Travis, "You better tell Mother."

He ran into the house and soon returned with her. She took one look at Snow White and said, "Send for Dr. Pritzker."

Now, sheep don't normally need any help having their babies. The front hooves come out first, and then the nose, as if they're diving headfirst into the world, and that's all there is to it. I knew this from reading Dr. Pritzker's books.

"Don't worry, Mother," I said, "it takes from one to four hours. There's plenty of time."

She stared at me. "How do you know that?"

"I, uh . . . heard it somewhere." She really didn't like me spending time at the vet's office, and she *really* wouldn't like the books I read there, some of them with stomach-turning pictures. Not ladylike, no, not at all.

"Travis," said Mother, "run for Dr. Pritzker."

"Really?" he said. "But she just started. Callie says there's lots of ti—"

Mother glared at him. "*Fetch* him, Travis, and *run*." Travis took off. Mother leaned over the railing, cooing soft words of encouragement. Snow White ignored her and kept straining to push the lamb out.

Twenty minutes went by with no progress. Mother grew more and more worked up.

"Where *is* that boy? Why is he so slow? We should have sent him on horseback."

"But then we'd have had to saddle a horse, and that would have taken at least—"

"Oh, do be quiet, Calpurnia." She started pacing and wringing her hands, something I'd only read about in books. She looked so tense, I felt sorry for her.

"It's all right, Mother. He'll be here shortly."

And right then we heard Travis

shouting "hello" from the end of the drive. He came pounding up, sweating and panting. And alone.

"Where is the doctor?" Mother nearly shouted. Travis and I both flinched. She almost never raised her voice.

Travis had to catch his breath before he could answer. "He's gone to see a horse at Holloways' farm."

"You silly boy, why didn't you go there? Go and get him this minute."

"Yes, Mother," he wheezed, then took off again at a slower pace. Poor Travis. The Holloways lived at the very far end of town.

"I'll get Dr. Pritzker his towel and bucket of water while we're waiting," I said.

Mother looked at me. "His what?"

"He always washes his hands in a bucket of warm water before and after he examines his patients. But we probably don't have to give him soap; he usually carries his own."

"How do you know that?"

Too late, I was already on my way to fetch the bucket and towel. I also grabbed a bar of soap, just in case.

Half an hour later, Dr. Pritzker pulled up the drive in his buggy with

Travis sitting next to him. He stopped in front of the house, and I ran to meet him.

"Hello, Calpurnia. Travis told me about your ewe. It doesn't sound that urgent to me. I've only got a few minutes; I have to get back to the Holloways. Their plow horse has got the colic. It's a real emergency. They can't afford to lose that horse."

"I think Mother just needs you to tell her that Snow White is okay. That sheep means a lot to her."

He nodded and collected his big leather bag of instruments. I led him to the pen where Snow White still strained and Mother still paced.

"Dr. Pritzker, thank heavens you're here."

"Calm yourself, Mrs. Tate. The domestic sheep is widely known as an easy birther. Very seldom does it require any help from man. Calpurnia, some soap and a bucket of water, if you please. Ah, I see you have them ready."

He carefully washed his hands. Just as he was drying them, Snow White gave an extra push, and out slid a tiny lamb. Easy as that.

"Oh, look," said Mother.

"Wow," said Travis.

Snow White nosed the lamb and licked it. It slowly wobbled to its feet.

"You see?" said Dr. Pritzker. "Nothing to it. Now if you'll excuse me, I must get back to my patient with colic." He packed up his tools.

Mother said, "Send us your bill, Doctor."

"Good heavens, Mrs. Tate, I did nothing to help. I can't send a bill on Mother Nature's behalf. No, no. I bid you good day."

I left Mother and Travis staring at the lamb and walked the vet back to his buggy. I gave his mare Penny a quick pat while he loaded up.

"Well, Calpurnia, is that the first lambing you've attended?"

"Yessir, although I've read all about it in your books."

He paused. "Have you now? Have you . . . uh . . . told your mother about your reading those books?"

Was he crazy? Mother would likely have a fit if she found out. "Never, Dr. Pritzker."

"Good. That's good. Your mother's a fine woman. No need to distress the dear lady." He climbed into the buggy, shook the reins, and clucked at Penny to giddyup. They took off at a trot.

7

I wandered back to the pen to admire the newborn with Mother and Travis as Snow White licked it clean.

Mother beamed. "That lamb will be worth quite a bit of money."

Travis looked alarmed. "You're not going to sell him, are you?"

"For wool, darling, not for meat. People all over town have been asking for Snow White's offspring for the wool."

"Oh. But he's awfully cute."

He *was* awfully cute. And I knew exactly what was coming next.

"Can't we keep him?" he said.

Mother ignored this. She knew that if we kept every animal Travis thought was cute, we'd be completely overrun with creatures of every sort, wild and tame, furred and finned and feathered.

"What shall we call him?" I said.

Mother thought for a moment.

"Snowball," she said. "Yes, I think that suits him, don't you?"

"Yes, that's good," said Travis. "Baby Snowball. Can I pat him, do you think?"

"Perhaps not yet, darling; give them a little time to get used to each other."

Snow White nuzzled her lamb and made low crooning noises. The lamb began to nurse, its tail wiggling like mad.

We stood and admired them in silence. Then something odd happened. Snow White stood up and stepped away from the lamb. Her soft crooning changed to a deep ugly grunt.

"What's wrong with her?" said Mother.

Travis squinted at her. "You know," he said slowly, "she's still kind of fat."

Of course! Why hadn't I seen it? Why hadn't Dr. Pritzker seen it? I guess he'd been in too much of a hurry. "I'll bet she's having twins," I said. "It happens all the time with sheep."

"Wonderful!" said Mother. "That's very good news."

Snow White paced around her pen. Baby Snowball baah-ed pitifully and struggled to follow her. She ignored him and kept on grunting and pacing.

Finally Mother said, "Is there . . . is there something wrong? The first one was so easy."

Yes, but twins had minds of their

own and didn't always come out the same way.

I stared at the patient and thought hard. What would Dr. Pritzker do if he were here? He'd told me many a time: First observe (look), then palpate (feel), and finally, act on the information you'd gathered.

"Travis," Mother said, "go and get Dr. Pritzker."

"He can't come," I said. "He's got an emergency at the Holloways'."

"Well," she said, "*this* is an emergency too."

Snow White lay down in the straw and grunted even louder.

I watched her closely. Why weren't the front hooves coming out? Where was the nose? As I watched, out came a strange-looking woolly puff. I stared at it in horror. It was the tail. The lamb was trying to come out backward, and it was stuck.

Mother took one look at my face and said, "Calpurnia, what's wrong?"

"It's backward," I muttered. "It's what they call a breech birth."

"Is that bad? That's bad, isn't it?"

Snow White grunted louder.

I told myself, *All right, Calpurnia, you think you're so smart. What about all that reading you've been doing at Dr. Pritzker's office? What good is it? Don't just stand there,* do *something.*

"Oh," said Mother, as if reading my thoughts, "somebody *do* something."

Travis had turned a faint greenish color, so no help there. Mother was back to wringing her hands again and looked like she might faint. So that left me. Okay.

I washed my hands in the bucket and dried them with the towel.

"What are you doing?" cried Mother.

"I think I know how to do this," I said, and climbed into the pen.

"Lord help us," Mother whispered.

Please do, I thought. *I need all the help I can get.* Baby Snowball kept pushing him-

self in the way, nuzzling at his mother.

"Travis," I said, "get this lamb out of here."

"Uh, what do you want me to do?"

"Just hold it," I snapped. "I can't do anything with it underfoot."

He reluctantly climbed in and pulled the lamb to the other side of the pen. Snowball started bleating. Louder and louder. It was amazing how much noise such a small organism could make.

I struggled to shut out the noise and think. All right. I closed my eyes for a second and tried to call up the page about breech births. Yes. There it was. You had to turn the lamb around. And the only way to turn it around was to push it back in. And then pull it out headfirst. If you couldn't turn it, it would never come out. And if it never came out, both mother and baby would die. And if they died, what was the use of all the studying I had done? What use was all the hard-won knowledge I was so proud of? Maybe I wasn't such a smart girl after all.

I gritted my teeth and pushed gently on the lamb.

"Are you mad?" cried Mother. "You've got to pull it *out*."

"I've got to push it in first to turn it around."

"Are you sure?" said Travis.

"How do you know?" said Mother.

I ignored her and pushed again. Snow White pushed back. I pushed harder this time and felt the lamb move a few inches up the birth canal.

"This can't be right," Mother said, fretting.

I pushed again, and Snow White squealed in protest. Or maybe pain. But I couldn't stop to think about that. The second lamb was now where I needed it.

"Quick, Travis, hand me that bit of twine behind you."

"What? Where?"

"Right behind you on the fence post. *Hurry.*"

He fumbled it to me, all the while trying to keep Snowball away.

I took the twine and made a loop in one end. Now came the tricky part. I

pushed the length of twine past the lamb and tried to snag one of the front hooves with it. The books made it sound so easy. Ha! I got it on about the eighth try. Slowly pushing the hind end away from me and pulling the

front hoof toward me with the twine, I felt the lamb turn to face me.

Yes! Here it came, the front hooves followed by the nose. I took hold of the hooves and pulled, and a moment later the lamb flopped out onto the straw headfirst as it was supposed to. But it lay completely still. It looked completely dead.

"You did it," shouted Travis.

"Good heavens," said Mother.

"Oh no," I said. Was it alive? Had I killed it with my clumsy doctoring? What made me think I could possibly—

One ear twitched.

"Look," said Travis.

A hind leg twitched.

"It's alive!" said Mother.

"Quick, Travis, hand me the towel."

I took the rough towel and started rubbing the lamb all over to get the circulation going. I wiped the mucus from its nose and mouth, and it took a deep gasping breath. Snow White looked at it and started crooning again.

A few minutes later, both lambs were up and nursing. Their mother munched happily on some fresh hay, turning every now and then to look with interest at these two new woolly bits of life.

I washed my hands in the bucket. And then something really strange happened. Little black spots danced before my eyes, and horrible prickly hives raced over my skin. My legs turned all rubbery and wouldn't hold me up. I sat down rather suddenly in the hay.

Mother said, "Are you all right?"

I took a few deep breaths. "Yes. At least . . . I think so." The little black spots danced away, and I slowly got to my feet.

Mother cleared her throat. "I think that's quite enough excitement for one day, don't you? Most . . . unexpected. I suppose that thanks are in order. So thank you, Calpurnia. That second lamb will be worth some extra money. Would you like to name it?"

Within me an idea bloomed, speaking at first in a tiny voice.

"No," I said, "Travis can name it."

"Gee, thanks, Callie," he said.

The idea grew and spoke louder to me. But did I dare say it aloud?

I did. I stared at my boots and said in a small voice, "I'd like to be paid."

Mother blinked at me. "What?"

"Paid. For my work."

The two of them gawked at me as if I'd suddenly started spouting a foreign language.

"Yes," I said louder. "I saved the mother. I saved the twin."

"I really don't understand where you get this idea of payment. Asking for cash is the height of unladylike behavior. I don't know how any daughter of mine ever—"

I couldn't believe it. I had just saved

her valuable livestock, and now she was going to lecture me on proper behavior. I fought to keep the anger out of my voice. "Then give me the twin. I saved it. I'll raise it. It should be mine."

She hesitated.

Travis said, "Yes, Mother, give her the lamb." He turned the full force of his best sunny smile on her. "That only seems fair. Don't you think so? Please?"

Mother wavered and then crumbled in the face of Travis's pleading.

"All right," she said. "I suppose you deserve it."

Ahh, the lamb was mine. I *was*

getting paid; that lamb would grow up to be worth a nice sum.

"What are you going to do with it?" said Travis. "You're not going to . . . to . . ."

"I think I'll sell it at auction in the fall. But don't worry, for wool, not for mutton."

"Oh, good," he said. "That's good. Can I still name it? Even though it's yours?"

"Of course you can."

"It should be called . . . Curly."

We looked at him in surprise. "Really?" I said.

"Don't you like it? It's a good name. It's a curly little lamb."

"I just thought you'd want to name it, oh, I don't know, Snowdrop or Snowflake or something like that."

"Nope. Curly."

So Curly it was.

Curly thrived, along with his brother, Snowball. His wool was every bit as fine as his mother's. I ended up selling him at the fall auction for the grand sum of $6.75. A fortune! All my brothers except for Travis moaned about how unfair it was.

And what did I do with the money?

Why, I ordered a fine magnifying glass of my very own from the Sears Catalogue so that I wouldn't have to keep borrowing Granddaddy's (not that he seemed to mind, but still). It came two weeks later, a beautiful heavy circle of glass with a bone handle packed snugly in its own leather box.

Suddenly the miniature world grew huge as I studied everything through it. A tiny beetle turned into a ferocious dragon; a blade of grass became a whole forest; a tadpole turned into a sea monster.

My brother Lamar, who had never

before shown any interest in Nature, took one envious look at my magnifier and groused, "I could have done it. I could have birthed that lamb, and then that money would be mine."

"Really?" I said. "I didn't see you standing there ready to catch any kind of lamb, Lamar, regular *or* breech."

"You were just lucky, that's all."

"Lucky? Ha! Granddaddy says you make your own luck. He says the more you know, the luckier you get. It's not about sheer chance, you see. It's about being ready."

Lamar, who had a nasty habit of

pulling braids and giving fierce pinches when no one was looking, said, "Well, then, are you ready for this?" and sprang at me. But I'd been watching him, and I was prepared. I jumped sideways and took off for the woods at top speed, knowing I could outfox him any day of the week. Because I was smarter. And faster. And readier. And luckier.